WHAT WOULD MAISIE DO?

Inspiration from the Pages of Maisie Dobbs

JACQUELINE WINSPEAR

HARPER PERENNIAL

An Imprint of HarperCollinsPublishers

HARPER PERENNIAL

HarperCollins books may be purchased for educational, business, or sales promotional use.
For information please email the Special Markets Department at SPsales@harpercollins.com.

FIRST EDITION

Designed by Nancy Leonard

Library of Congress Cataloging-in-Publication Data has been applied for.

ISBN 978-0-06-285934-1

19 20 21 22 23 SCP 10 9 8 7 6 5 4 3 2 1

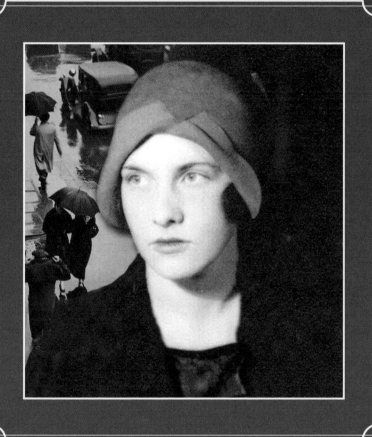

WHAT WOULD MAISIE DO?

I t was soon after *Maisie Dobbs*—the first novel in the series featuring psychologist and investigator Maisie Dobbs—was published that I began to receive emails and letters from readers who were intrigued by the "wisdom" within the pages, especially the continued advice offered to Maisie by her longtime mentor, Dr. Maurice Blanche. I confess, I had to read through the book again to find those passages readers especially loved. I am like many writers in that much of the narrative and dialogue in my novels goes straight to the page without interference from my conscious mind! I have an idea of the overall arc of the story, but so much between the beginning, middle and end is down to inspiration and determination.

The positive comments from readers continued, and by the third book in the series, *Pardonable Lies*, people were letting me know they were keeping notes on certain phrases and sections of dialogue that resonated with them. I heard from a number of psychologists working with veterans and those suffering the slings and arrows of a difficult period in life—apparently they were recommending the books to their patients. I suspected the key was not only the wise Maurice Blanche, but Maisie Dobbs and those in her circle; they were characters who had lived through the worst of times, a time of terrible war. They had encountered personal problems that had to be endured, and the qualities of resilience and persistence were an important feature in the narrative of each book. Perhaps that was it.

As time has passed—and as I write this book, I am also working on the fifteenth novel in the series—I have encountered even more readers who are keeping tabs on what one reader summed up as "the big sister I never had—someone there to support me and advise me." Another reader told me, "When I'm stuck in life, I ask myself, 'What would Maisie do?'"

That was the catalyst for me to begin putting together a compendium of short passages from the Maisie Dobbs series—to inspire, to encourage deeper consideration of a problem, to soften a blow or to give insight into another's feelings, perhaps. And along the way I've added my own interpretations, as well as blank journal pages for you to mull over those words, make your own notes and perhaps add favorite lines I've omitted. I hope you enjoy asking yourself "What would Maisie do?" as much as I have enjoyed bringing this book to you.

I wish you well,
Jacqueline
August 2018

HOW TO USE THIS BOOK

What Would Maisie Do? is more than a journal, more than an accompaniment to a series of historical novels; I envisaged it to be a living document. And to take something from the life of psychologist and investigator Maisie Dobbs, *What Would Maisie Do?* could also be seen as your personal "case map."

As a guideline, I would urge you to remember the counsel Maisie received from her mentor, Dr. Maurice Blanche: "Stay with the question." Each quote from one of the novels is followed by notes giving insight into my inspiration for the passage and closes with a question or two for you to consider. There is no need to fill the page with your response at once, nor is there a requirement for you to work through the journaling part of *What Would Maisie Do?* in a linear fashion. You can pick and choose from each section, making notes and possibly adding your own questions along the way. I would also urge you to take a leaf from Maisie's book and allow yourself the gift of silence as you read and consider each passage—with a caveat, and that is to also consider the power of conversation.

I remember, years ago, when I was in school, an English teacher telling us that the root of the word "conversation" had to do with more than communicating together; it meant the "act of living with" others and as such suggests the process of learning in community. I like the latter idea, that we can learn in company and conversation with others. So how might it be if you gathered with a group of friends, perhaps other readers of the Maisie Dobbs novels, to consider and discuss each section in *What Would Maisie Do?* Share your thoughts and feelings in a safe environment, where a commitment to honor the privacy of the group is made and there is a code of confidentiality. Writing might be part of what happens in company. Or later, when alone again, the earlier conversation might inspire insights you are ready to record in your journal. You will see there are pages not only for recording your responses at the end of each section, but also at the end of the book, where you can add quotes from the series that have not been included—again, you could share those passages with your group, describing why they have a special meaning for you.

Any journal is dynamic. It asks you to hold up a mirror to the self, as Maurice has done so many times with Maisie. In turn, as she proceeds through an investigation, Maisie will use questions to hold up a mirror to those who cross her path, often as they make the pilgrimage through a period of chaos.

I wish you well as you rediscover the Maisie Dobbs series from another perspective, and I thank you, dear readers, for inspiring this book. As I created the character of Maisie Dobbs, and as she revealed herself to me, I wanted her to embody the qualities of endurance, resilience, empathy, kindness and perspective. I wanted her to learn and grow from experience, to make mistakes and have good days and bad days, and, ultimately, to be a reflection of what it is to be human. In working your measured way through *What Would Maisie Do?*— perhaps alone or in community with others—you'll learn not only more about Maisie Dobbs, but about yourself.

"Stay with the question. The more it troubles you, the more it has to teach you. In time, Maisie, you will find that the larger questions in life share such behavior."

—MAISIE DOBBS

A QUESTION OF POWER

From childhood, it seems we're taught that the whole point of having a question leveled at us is to respond immediately with an answer. We rush to react to emails and requests, many of them beginning with "Can you . . . ?" "Would you . . . ?" "What do you think?" And then there are the questions we put to ourselves—and sometimes try to silence almost as soon as they emerge. Questions such as "What is it about this person that unsettles me?" or "Why do I feel such discomfort?" or "What should I do about this?"

In an age of instant gratification, it's easy to succumb to the habit of blasting out an answer before we've thought about the question, before we've allowed it to settle into us, and before we've had time to turn it around and bring all the knowledge we've garnered throughout our lives to bear upon our response. Society doesn't help us along the way, pressing the agendas of others upon us, often while undermining what could be a powerful process of coming to an awareness of what action to take in a given situation. Phrases such as "Oh, you must know what to do—you've been in this job for years!" (or similar) pressure us into answering questions in a speedy fashion, and we are often our own worst enemy, admonishing ourselves with an inner dialogue that sounds something like this: "I'll look stupid/silly/ ill-informed/unprofessional if I say I need more time to think about it."

Maurice taught Maisie that the power of a question lies not in the answer, but in the process we go through to arrive at our answer. It's in what we learn along the way, and it is in the attention we pay to our responses, to the conclusions we draw as we come to our summing-up. It is as if we were looking at an ordinary pebble in the palm of our hand, having been asked what color it is. "Beige," we might say. But then we look closer, hold the pebble to the light, and we see threads of purple, gray, blue and red, and we come to know something of ourselves, that perhaps the answer to the question is as multifaceted as our own character.

What does this mean in practical terms? Yes, without doubt there are times when a snap decision must be made, but in that instance we draw upon information available to us at the time, and we trust our response is the best we could have made with that knowledge. But other questions that do not need or seem to ask for an instant answer? Take your time. Ask for time. As if Maurice Blanche has given you leave to do so, give yourself the opportunity to see all the threads of color in the nugget of inquiry, and perhaps learn something of yourself and your world along the way.

Has there been an occasion when you've felt pressured to answer a question? How did you feel? And how might you have claimed more time to draw upon your resources to answer the question? Consider your response, tucking those thoughts away to support you should a similar situation arise in the future.

"My child, when a mountain appears on the journey,
we try to go to the left, then to the right. We try to find
the easy way to navigate our way back to the easier path.
But the mountain is there to be crossed. It is on that
pilgrimage, as we climb higher, that we are forced to shed
the layers upon layers we have carried for so long.
Then we find that our load is lighter and we have come
to know something of ourselves in the perilous climb. . . .
Do not seek to avoid the mountain, my child, for it has
been placed there at a perfect time. It will only become larger
if you seek to delay or draw back from the ascent."

—PARDONABLE LIES

ASCENDING LIFE'S MOUNTAINS

I n this passage, Maisie Dobbs is the beneficiary of the many years of wisdom held within the heart and mind of Khan, the elderly man who had once been mentor to Dr. Maurice Blanche. Khan describes a process that we all have a tendency to adopt when faced with a problem, a mountain on life's journey: We do our best to avoid it. Perhaps we avoid confrontation or we hold in our emotions when faced with a challenge. We might turn away from opportunity, wondering what we might risk if we reach beyond our comfort zone. The mountain can take many forms, and most of us have had experience in trying to avoid the climb—which may involve making peace with someone or moving to another location. Perhaps we even move to another place to avoid the mountain!

The point is we all know the mountain when it looms into view, and we've probably all done our best to avoid it. At the heart of our avoidance is most likely fear—and that fear is inextricably linked to what we believe we might lose as we embark upon the climb. Yet as the passage indicates, we *have* to lose layers as we climb, as we persevere through the challenge of ascent. Layers of fears, perhaps even of a deeply held grudge, must be jettisoned to make us lighter as we continue our pilgrimage. Sometimes it's necessary for us to quite literally lose our belongings, our material possessions, casting them aside as we climb the mountain, knowing they serve us no longer.

Every challenge we encounter is an opportunity to reconsider who we are, what we stand for, and how we can honor the very best of ourselves as we turn away from the easy way out. The challenge—the climb—represents a pilgrimage, and a pilgrimage always holds within it the promise of greater self-knowledge. Maisie is being counseled not to draw back from a mountain that has appeared on her journey, for she can only learn and become more whole during the ascent.

Maisie might ask you to describe a mountain you have conquered. She would want to know what you learned about yourself along the way, and what you had to cast aside and leave behind forever to come to this place of accomplishment. You can write about it here.

And it occurred to her that she was so used to turning over everything in her mind, as if each thought were an intricate shell found at the beach, that she had never truly known the value in simply accepting things as they were.

—ELEGY FOR EDDIE

THE VALUE
OF ACCEPTANCE

Maisie Dobbs is the sort of person who tends to consider aspects of her life and work in great detail. Today we might come to the conclusion that she is an "overthinker." But that's also part of her work, her training—and there's a lot to be said for a deeper inquiry into certain aspects of life before making important decisions, or jumping to conclusions about a person or situation. But as Maisie comes to learn, life is sometimes best experienced from a place of acceptance, taking aspects of life as they are, rather than picking them apart to see if we can arrange them differently—after all, change one thing, and you might find that a lot of things have to be altered to accommodate the first decision, to make elements of life fit together again.

As a writer, and as the creator of Maisie Dobbs, I have often drawn upon personal experience and observation in the development of characters or situations—it's something all writers do, which is why we go everywhere with a notebook tucked away in an inside pocket or a backpack. The lessons inherent in acceptance—and the challenge of accepting a situation—tend to come along at different intervals in life. There's the unexpected change in circumstances that we believe we could have held some dominion over—those are the ones that can haunt us, as they have Maisie on occasion. This came home to me during the year I began to write *Maisie Dobbs*. I had a very serious accident while I was out riding my horse. The accident resulted in multiple injuries, which effectively incapacitated me for a few months. One of my friends gave me this advice in the days before surgery to mend my seriously broken arm and shoulder. "You've got to just accept what has happened and get on with it," he said. "If you go back over every single decision that led to that moment of the accident, you'll never get better. You'll always be in that moment of the accident, asking yourself why you chose to ride that day, why you went through that gate, why you galloped up that hill. Stop turning it all over and consider nothing but getting well again."

I think that's the kind of advice Maisie would offer, though we know she might also be challenged to follow it.

And I should add that I took my friend's advice, and instead of wallowing in what had come to pass, I finished my first novel.

Can you remember a time when you were challenged to accept an uncomfortable situation? Or perhaps you fought against the inevitable and caused yourself unnecessary discomfort? What have you learned about the practice of acceptance?

Maisie's father, Frankie Dobbs, would have brought his horse and cart to Covent Garden every day to stock up with fruit and vegetables to take on his rounds as a costermonger.

"Listen and attend to the ear of your heart, Maisie."

—LEAVING EVERYTHING MOST LOVED

LISTENING
WITH THE HEART

Now we come to one of my favorite characters, Dame Constance Charteris, the Benedictine nun who was once one of Maisie's tutors during her years at university, but who is now the abbess of Camden Abbey, set among the lands of Romney Marsh in Kent. Dame Constance challenges Maisie—and in truth, this is why Maisie returns to her when she needs someone to act as devil's advocate, countering her thoughts on a given subject. In this scene Dame Constance is reminding Maisie to listen to that voice within and to follow her heart's desire—and she has quoted from the Rule of St. Benedict to underline her point: "Listen and attend to the ear of your heart."

There have been several translations of this simple yet meaning-ful sentence. Some suggest it is "*attend with* the ear of your heart," and others maintain that it is "*incline to* the ear of your heart." Each translation gives us food for thought. It asks us to listen to others with our hearts, paying attention to them, bringing the very best of ourselves to the act of listening, respectful of their humanity.

But there is a deeper meaning, and one that is directed at Maisie in the conversation. The advice from Dame Constance asks Maisie to take the course of action her heart tells her is right; it asks her to follow the counsel of her best, most loving self. For what is the heart, if not the place where love resides?

Dame Constance takes the teaching of St. Benedict and challenges Maisie to listen deeply to the wisdom already held inside, which is the result of all she has learned and come to know across the years of her life. In listening to the ear of her heart, Maisie can, with grace and compassion, move forward, for even on the most solitary pilgrimage, she will not be alone.

What does "listening with the ear of the heart" mean to you? Recount a situation where you truly listened to your heart's counsel before taking action. Describe how that felt, and what you might have learned as a result.

. . . .

. . . .

. . . .

. . . .

. . . .

. . . .

. . . .

. . . .

. . . .

The quote on the opposite page was used as an epigraph to introduce a book in the Maisie Dobbs series, and has proved to be a favorite with readers. If it resonates with you, write about it here.

❄

....
....
....
....
....
....
....
....
....
....
....
....
....
....
....
....
....
....
....
....
....
....
....
....

Pilgrimage to the place of the wise is to
find escape from the flame of separateness.

—JAL L AD-D N AR-R M

Maurice had spoken to her, more than once, about the importance of seeking distinctions when asking others to describe their feelings, or when trying to identify emotions in the self. At first she had not understood, and now, her eyes closed, she recalled the moment, the conversation when he said to her, "To just say, 'I'm sad,' isn't enough. To gain greater understanding of the situation, of yourself or another, you must search for a word that better describes the moment. Sometimes we say we're sad when we would be better served by using the word melancholy, for example. . . . The distinction helps us identify a path through the maze of emotion—and emotions can be debilitating, can paralyze us if we allow them power, and we do that when we fail to be precise. It's rather like accruing knowledge of your enemy so that you can defeat him. So, Maisie, how do you feel?"

—ELEGY FOR EDDIE

ON THE POWER OF DISTINCTION

'm sure we've all come across this lesson at some point in school or college—that of seeking distinction in language. But perhaps we've not reflected upon the lesson since, either in our communication with others or in terms of our inner dialogue. Often in conversation we will use the simplest word because we don't have the time—or patience, perhaps—to consider a word choice that better reflects our meaning or intention.

Given that so much human anguish is caused by less-than-accurate communication, it's worth us considering the importance of distinction. And it could be argued that in not exercising distinction in our listening, we are also setting ourselves up for disappointment. For example, how many times does our inability, for whatever reason, to express emotional pain become anger and annoyance?

In this passage, Maisie is encouraged to seek distinction in order to better understand another person, to bring compassion and deeper thought to consideration of the human condition. Given that Maisie is being tasked to make distinctions, how might greater attention to our words and thoughts affect our relationships and our experiences, personally and professionally, each and every day? How might you have been more distinct in a given conversation—even if that dialogue was with yourself?

If we ask "What would Maisie do?" I believe she would compile a list of all the words she uses to describe her feelings, observations about people, and responses to good or bad situations and would find she tends to fall back on the same words, as we all seem to do. Her next step would be to list other words that might have better served her in a given circumstance. Are there words you use repeatedly to describe an emotion or situation?

···

···

···

···

···

···

···

···

···

···

···

···

···

"Everything yields to pressure, Maisie," Maurice had
taught her. *"The slow drip of water on stone will, in
time, wear away a ridge. Even the strongest metal,
if enough weight is applied, will start to bend. Some
cases will begin to give quickly. But do not despair
of the assignment when it seems to defy every effort.
Just give it time. Continue with your work, with your
questions and observations. Wait for the yielding."*

—TO DIE BUT ONCE

THE YIELDING TO SUSTAINED EFFORT

Ah, another piece of sage advice from Maurice Blanche that seems to suggest patience. Yet, there's more to it than simply the notion of waiting. The power of endurance underpins this passage. As a writer, I learned this lesson as I wrote my first novel, and I learn it again and again when I'm in the midst of crafting another story and the dreaded doubt creeps in. Every writer spends time in the doldrums, hoping the wind will pick up and fill the sails again. It always does, but the key is that you have to keep writing. It's no good thinking that just because today is not filled to the brim with inspiration, you can give up and walk away from the task until it comes back again. Writers who finish novels—people who complete any project—know that you have to continue on. The water has to keep dripping onto the cold, hard stone.

I have seen people give up a dearly held dream—be it a creative project, a transition into a new career or saving for something they would love to own—because they have not tapped into their ability to endure. A hallmark of Maisie Dobbs' character is her resilience and her ability to persevere through the most troubling times. Life's challenges have burnished the metal in her character, with each lesson providing her with proof of her ability to reach the other side of life's challenges. She does not have supernatural powers, but instead she has learned to harness even the slightest breeze to carry her through those doldrums—and so she moves on, setting her sails, trusting the yielding.

For all of us there have been times when we have had to "Keep Calm and Carry On." Times when we have had to demonstrate radical trust that all will be well, that like drops of water on stone our efforts will come to fruition. Reflecting on our inner resources—those qualities of endurance and resilience—reminds us of our strengths and that they are there for us to harness when needed. Make some notes here to remind yourself of times when you have had to keep going, applying pressure until the yielding began.

The borough of Lambeth
during Maisie's childhood.

ON LOCATION

Lambeth

Maisie Dobbs was born and grew up in what is now the London borough of Lambeth. However, on my grandmother's birth certificate—she, too, was born in Lambeth—the borough is identified as being in the county of Surrey, which indicates how London has encroached outward over the centuries. Despite the borough containing some grand houses and having connections to the Church of England—Lambeth Palace, the official residence of the Archbishop of Canterbury, is in north Lambeth—most residents experienced great poverty in the 1800s.

The London borough of Lambeth now includes the parishes of Kennington, Vauxhall, Waterloo, South Lambeth, Stockwell, Brixton, Denmark Hill, Herne Hill, Tulse Hill, Streatham and West Norwood. All of these areas have known times of boom and bust, with so many of the large mansions—many now divided into flats—having been built by wealthy merchants who traded in goods from overseas and needed to be within striking distance of the River Thames and its famous docks, yet preferred to reside near some of the more parklike settings of Lambeth. But by the mid-1800s, the borough began to grow quickly; from fewer than twenty-eight thousand residents in 1801, Lambeth's population had increased to more than three hundred thousand in 1901. Such expansion did not come without problems, especially at a time when so many agricultural workers were moving into the cities to take advantage of jobs in factories that came with the Industrial Revolution. They had left farm life behind for a different kind of toil—and fled the seeming drudgery of rural life often to find great poverty and sickness in the overcrowded city. One vintage photograph (not available here) sticks in my mind, of a group of children at school in early 1900s Lambeth. Not one child was wearing a pair of shoes.

Maisie's father worked hard to ensure that she had shoes on her feet and remained in school for as long as she could (the average age of those leaving school was twelve in those days, though many children were absent from classes at a much younger age, running errands and working in the factories to contribute to the family finances). Maisie's lowly beginnings, along with those key qualities of perseverance and endurance that bring people through the worst of times, have grounded her throughout her life—but they have also been her Achilles' heel, especially when life has seemed to favor her with gifts.

When you look back on your own childhood, no matter what the circumstances of the years of your growing, what gifts were you given, simply by being young in a certain place at a certain time?

The quote on the opposite page was used as an epigraph to introduce a book in the Maisie Dobbs series, and has proved to be a favorite with readers. If it resonates with you, write about it here.

....
....
....
....
....
....
....
....
....
....
....
....
....
....
....
....
....
....
....
....
....
....
....
....

He who gives up the smallest part of a secret
has the rest no longer in his power.

—JEAN PAUL RICHTER, *TITAN*

"It's a web, though."

"I deal with them every day.
Dr. Blanche gave us sage advice
in order to untangle them.
Patience, and one thread at a time."

—TO DIE BUT ONCE

ABOUT PATIENCE

As a psychologist and investigator, Maisie Dobbs is always facing one kind of web or another, yet from her early days as apprentice to Dr. Maurice Blanche, she has been tutored in the power of the somewhat deliberate art of investigation, unraveling a mass of tangled evidence by following the thread of each clue, each lead with care and attention.

Longtime readers of the Maisie Dobbs series have observed the many references to fabrics, threads and yarns throughout the novels. It will therefore come as no surprise to learn that I studied textile art for several years, working with all forms of fabric and thread. It's a very tactile process of creating an image, especially when working on a large loom and following the warp and weft threads to ensure there are no errors in the tapestry. It came very easily for me, as I crafted each story, to use wools, silks, cottons and even wood, metal, leaves and stone as metaphors for something else. Shaping a narrative seemed so akin to creating textile art. Day after day I not only constructed webs, but had to follow threads with care so as not to ruin an entire piece because something was in the wrong place! Patience was of the essence, as it always is in writing.

Those hours at the loom and with a mass of off-cut fabrics I was using to create a collage gave me a lesson worth learning: that the tangles presented to us in life often require close attention and patience to unravel, as we pull threads away to find clarity and release knots from our line. Those tangles can appear at work, in personal relationships, in any of life's domains—they can happen in an instant, yet can only be unraveled with time.

As a child I always wanted to solve problems quickly and often managed to get myself into a huge mess as I threw myself into sorting out a problem, whether it was mending my bike or finding the solution to a challenge in my homework. I just wanted to get things done, finished. The advice in this passage—and in the guidance given to Maisie Dobbs—mirrors my father's counsel to me, and on many occasions, I might add! "Don't be rush-headed. Take your time. Study the problem, look at it from different angles, and you will be able to solve it." Given that he had been an explosives expert during the war, it's probably fair to say my father's approach was inspired by the reality of his job—if he was "rush-headed," he could have been killed. Yet how often have we been wounded by our impatience?

What I learned, too, was that patience paid off. Every time I was faced with lines of threads that I had to unpick, the words "more haste, less speed" seemed to echo in my head.

Is there a situation where a more patient approach to a problem might have served you? And what nuggets can you take from this passage that resonate in your life?

"Coincidence is a messenger sent by truth."

—MAISIE DOBBS

PAYING ATTENTION TO COINCIDENCE

This quote comes up time and again in the Maisie Dobbs series. It first appeared as counsel offered to Maisie by her mentor, Dr. Maurice Blanche. As a writer, often words and phrases emerge and I have no idea where they came from—and I know all writers experience this phenomenon. I might be working at my desk writing a scene, and at once I'll look back at a phrase and think, *Now where on earth did that come from?* And of course I know that it comes from a well of observations made not only during my research, but throughout my life. (I have a theory that writers start life as quietly observant or very nosy children—perhaps both!)

The sense that there is more to coincidence is something I have paid attention to since childhood, whether inspired by an idle thought about a friend who a minute later is knocking at the door, or reading about someone and then another person mentions her. And we've all had the experience of a loved one coming into our thoughts, and then the phone rings and it's that person calling us. Coincidence is a big part of life, and I believe that for an investigator—especially one such as Maisie Dobbs, who has a finely tuned sense of intuition—

coincidence will always be a signal for her to stop, to consider the synchronicity of the event and to pay attention.

I have found it useful to take a second look at coincidences in my own life. If three people happen to say the same thing to me, I consider it fair warning, a truth worthy of my attention. It might be something as simple as a book recommendation or an event I might be interested in. And you can bet that if it has to do with travel, then I am all ears!

To an investigator, a coincidence—that serendipitous moment—is a fateful message, a pointing of the finger in a certain direction, and it should not be ignored.

How might it be if we were all alert to those fortuitous moments of coincidence, stopping to pay attention and even to act upon the direction a coincidence appears to suggest? If I think of someone in my circle and another friend mentions her, then without ado I will contact that person. Years ago I had a dream about a friend I had not seen in years, and then—by coincidence, perhaps—I was going through old documents and letters and I found a Christmas card from her. That was enough for me to do the little research required to find a current email address. The reply I received was one expressing such gratitude, because she was going through a very difficult time and as a result was feeling isolated and without support.

We all have those moments, those opportunities to take coincidence more seriously. Maurice effectively gave Maisie permission to indulge her curiosity and to follow the threads of coincidence as they appear. Time and again she finds coincidence allied to truths that aid her in her work.

Are you aware of coincidences in your life? How do you treat them? As something to be considered and possibly acted upon? Has paying attention to coincidence ever aided you in some way? Maisie would urge you to reflect upon what happened, and suggest you begin to make a note of coincidences and what truths they've revealed in your life.

....
....
....
....
....
....
....
....
....
....
....
....
....
....
....
....
....
....

*There were no family photographs, no small framed portraits
on the mantelpiece over the fire in the sitting room as there
were at her father's house. She thought the flat would be all
the better for some photographs, not only to serve as reminders
of those who were loved, or reflections of happy times spent
in company, but to act as mirrors, where she might see
the affection with which she was held by those dear to her.
A mirror in which she could see her connections.*

—AMONG THE MAD

THE IMPORTANCE
OF PHOTOGRAPHS

I f the emails and letters I receive from readers are anything to go by, this passage is a favorite among fans of the Maisie Dobbs series. If you've read all the novels in the series, you will know that photographs feature quite frequently as Maisie goes about her work. She pays attention to a portrait on the wall, a series of family snaps arranged upon a mantelpiece or an image of a long-lost love, framed in silver and kept by a bedside. In an age of almost narcissistic obsession with selfies, the power of the photograph in years past can be easily overlooked.

Photographs connect us to an event, a time and place, and to those who have played a part in our lives—be it a beloved family member or a passing stranger; a son's wedding or a daughter departing for university. Dogs, humans, horses, places and events—they are all there to be recorded. Every picture tells a story, and we know that Maisie considers an image of a person and sees the look in their eyes revealing an emotion they have tried to conceal or the stance that tells of weariness, fear, joy or love. But in *Among the Mad*, she sees something more in the power of a photograph—the way in which it is a mirror, a reflection upon who we are and our connection to others.

I was inspired to write about the power of photographs by the many visits I have made to the home of my oldest friends. We have known each other since childhood, and through the years their "rogues' gallery" (as I have called it) has grown to take up significant space in their home. In every room there's a collage or two: photos of new babies welcomed into the family, first school days recorded, holidays with family and friends, weddings, days out at home and overseas. Then there are more new babies, the next generation spreading branches of family and loved ones rooted in one marriage. Along the way I can find myself in that tale—as a schoolgirl, then as a friend catching a bouquet, holding my goddaughter as a babe in arms, and later, that same child, now married, holding out her firstborn for me to take. It occurred to me, then, that photographs are a mirror in which we see ourselves connected—and for Maisie, in her isolation as *Among the Mad* unfolds, it is a powerful realization.

I believe that if Maisie were to talk to you about your family and friends, she might ask you: How do you hold your connections dear?

. . . .
. . . .
. . . .
. . . .
. . . .

Fitzroy Square, London, where
Maisie Dobbs's office is located.

ON LOCATION

Fitzroy Square, London

S ince *Maisie Dobbs* was first published in 2003 and began to accumulate a veritable legion of fans, I've received so many messages from readers recounting trips to England, where they have embarked upon what I will call the "Maisie Dobbs Trail," visiting many of the places mentioned in the novels. And I have received quite a few emails with "In Fitzroy Square!" as the subject line and a photograph attached of a smiling reader holding a copy of *Maisie Dobbs* while standing next to the Fitzroy Square sign. It's great fun to receive those messages.

I chose Fitzroy Square as the location for Maisie's office because I used to work in Conway Street, overlooking the square and just along from J. Evans, the old dairy building, which in the late 1970s was still a small grocery store where the owners lived over the shop. I remember telling one of my parents' neighbors where I was working and was met with the comment, "Not a particularly salubrious area." Of course, that summing-up made its way into *Maisie Dobbs*, with the words spoken by Lady Rowan Compton.

Another reason for choosing the square was its history, because it was known as an area where "a peer could sit next to a plumber at supper." Nowadays, the area is known as Fitzrovia, though no one ever referred to it as such when I worked there—it would have sounded far too posh—yet the name is said to have originated in the 1930s. Author Mike Pentelow, who cowrote *Characters of Fitzrovia* (Chatto & Windus, 2001), described the area around Fitzroy Square: "The wide variety of characters who mixed informally and easily as equals is what most fascinated me about Fitzrovia when I first moved into the area in 1972, and why I have stayed in it ever since." As a writer of character-driven novels, why would I want to situate my protagonist anywhere else? And as if to underline my choice, Pentelow goes on to say in his book:

Where else would Karl Marx and Prince Eddy (in direct line of accession to the throne) have gone to meetings about 20 yards apart? Or in the 1930s a cabinet minister and a road sweeper have attended the same wedding reception in the Fitzroy Tavern? Or, more recently, the Duke of Kent and a local homeless street-dweller have eaten in the same Charlotte Street restaurant?

Many of the old, famous restaurants were still in the area when I worked in Fitzroy Square. Maisie has eaten at Schmidt's and Bertorelli's, while Billy Beale is known to drop into one of the local pubs for a swift half-pint before going home. None of Maisie's neighbors would have batted an eyelid at the motley assortment of people who have made their way to her door—from Scotland Yard detectives to Covent Garden costermongers, from debutantes to spies. I think even Virginia Woolf, who lived in Fitzroy Square from 1907 to 1911, would have passed without making comment. It was, after all, at 29 Fitzroy Square that members of the Bloomsbury Group met for their Thursday evening salons.

It had always interested her, that physically gazing out at a landscape, even if that landscape offered a cluster of town buildings, could provide a broader view of the possibilities inspired by a question. She did the same thing herself, when something troubled her.

—TO DIE BUT ONCE

THE POWER
OF LANDSCAPE

Many of us underestimate the link between how we think and our physical being, especially when navigating our way through a problem, wrestling with a question or enduring a troubling period in life. So often it's tempting to hunker down, shut oneself away or find that place of comfort to console ourselves until—we hope—the clouds of our unknowing part and the light of resolution shines through.

Maurice has always counseled Maisie to "move the body," for in moving the body, we also move the mind. I learned this in a very practical sense when I was a child. My mother and father were of the opinion that any problem was easier solved during and after a long walk. If I came home and complained about something happening at school that bothered me, I was sent out to take the dog for a walk across the fields. And it seemed to work—all the negative feelings that had become glued together and unmovable in my mind were suddenly breaking down as I approached the problem with a more positive attitude.

In later years, I brought what I had learned into my life coaching practice, and though much of my work was done via telephone, if possible I would meet my client and hike to the top of a hill or another place with an expansive view, and without fail, the responses to questions came with greater ease, deeper insight and increased optimism. In moving the body, it seemed the mind could more easily grasp the power of possibility.

Try this: Next time you encounter a problem, or a difficult question is presented to you, don't fret about it at home within the confines of your four walls—take yourself to a place with a view. This can be done as easily in a town or city as it can in the country. Look about you as you turn that question over in your mind. Answers may not necessarily come in thick and fast, but the act of moving, of going to another place and shifting your body—and your vision—will impact your responses to the questions that seem unanswerable. Write about your experiences here.

Maurice had taught her that silencing the mind
was a greater task than stilling the body.

—MAISIE DOBBS

STILLING THE
BODY—AND THE MIND

Thisis lesson from Maurice Blanche is yet another that was inspired by personal experience, though I know I am not the only person on the planet who finds stilling the mind a challenge! Yet as I discovered, once the noise in the mind is silenced—or, at the very least, wound down a few decibels—it's possible to be more attuned to the wisdom we hold inside: the "knowing" about what is best for us in a given situation.

Many years ago, long before I began writing *Maisie Dobbs*, I decided to go on a silent retreat. A dearly loved cousin had died, and I felt I needed time alone—and not the sort of alone you might experience just by turning off the phone or not answering the door. I went to a retreat at a hermitage on the California coast so that I might spend three days in complete solitude. No laptop. No TV or radio. No phone. And the rule was strict: No talking to anyone else, even if you saw them on the trail. I thought I had slipped into my cell of aloneness quite easily—until the racket in my head started, as if my brain wanted to party because the whole house was too quiet. I felt as if I could physically hear the noise my thoughts made, but I persevered. I kept my silence. I sat alone in my room or in the garden looking up at the Milky Way, waiting for the noise to stop. Then there came the point where even the crashing waves seemed to recede into the distance, until I could hear what mystics have called the "still, small voice within." I did not strain to hear, but simply did my best to gather myself into the silence.

In many ways it was a life-changing experience. I am usually one of those people for whom meditation is a challenge. My mind goes off on a tangent, and I begin to think about work or what to have for dinner, whether I remembered to give the dog her meds or if I locked the door when I left the house. But here's what I learned having silenced my mind: how simply sweet that inner voice can be. Perhaps there is an indication of this in nature, for the sweetest part of the bloom is deep inside, beyond the noise and flourish of color.

When the retreat ended, I drove back to "civilization" very slowly. The sounds of everyday life—cars, phones, people talking, ATMs beeping with every screen touch—were an assault on me physically and spiritually.

We can't all just go off on silent retreats—in fact, that was the only one I have ever experienced—but we can try to create a mini-escape from the exterior noise and the constant hum that muffles the small voice within.

Even at the most demanding of times, Maisie will pull a cushion off the sofa and sit on the floor. She will close her eyes to the world. Five minutes. Ten minutes. It might not be long, but she dips into the well of silence to access the counsel of her inner knowing.

Can you find time for a personal retreat of even just a few minutes? What can you put to one side to hear the priceless truth that lies within you?

....
....
....
....
....
....
....
....
....
....
....
....
....
....
....
....
....
....
....

ABOUT CLOTHING, MOTOR CARS, AND A SENSE OF TIME AND PLACE

There's a reason I detail elements of life such as clothing, cars and food in the Maisie Dobbs series, and it has to do with giving the reader a sense of time and place, along with underlining aspects of character. From the very first introduction to Maisie Dobbs, readers know she does not wear brand-new clothes—indeed, in reality, who does? On any one day I might be wearing a two-year-old sweater, possibly over a T-shirt that has seen better times, and jeans from a good five years ago. Rarely does anyone go out with all items of clothing brand new, unless they're going to a special event. Even a bride wears something "old" along with "something new, something borrowed and something blue" on her big day. Maisie has always been reticent about treating herself to new clothing, so she is not exactly up-to-the-minute with regard to fashion, and this gives us some insight to her character, though that insight is often provided by her friend Priscilla Partridge, who is apt to try to nudge Maisie into more stylish and colorful garments. Priscilla is a fashion plate and, over the years, has made some pointed comments about Maisie's clothing choices—and those conversations also give insight into the relationship between the two women.

Cars become important in historical fiction, because we are so used to the electronic ignition, as well as other conveniences in automobile technology, we forget that before about 1929, most cars would not start with just a turn of the key and required switching on the gasoline supply—"petrol" in the UK—and then physically turning a handle at the front of the car to start the engine. You had to open the window to signal your turns by hand at all times, because even if a car had an automatic turn signal, it was likely of the semaphore type and could hardly be seen. Indeed, even language is important, because the abbreviation of "motor car" in Britain gives a sense of time, as most people shortened the term to "motor" and not "car" in those days. All these choices made by the writer of an historical novel are not due simply to a love of clothing or cars, but to a desire to enhance the reader's immersion into the time period and the story.

Do you recall favorite clothing worn by your grandparents or parents? These memories link us to the past and to our heritage, so it's always fun to remember and talk about them. Automobiles are important too—I know most families have a story of a car that seemed to have a mind of its own or a road trip that didn't quite live up to expectations. Those experiences become part of our mythology, the stories that bind us, so it's important to remember and record them.

Fenwick

OF BOND STREET
(CORNER OF BROOK STREET)

Special showing of Spring fashions to celebrate the OPENING OF NEW EXTENDED PREMISES.

WITH a superb ground-floor Showroom —almost doubling the previous selling space . . . these bigger premises allow an even wider service in all departments. Please come TO-DAY and see the fascinating collection of Frocks, Hats, Sportswear and Tailor-mades . . . Clothes that are graceful and gay—expressive of Youth and its needs of the moment.

This Three-Piece is of finest Chiffon Tweed Stockinette. The long - sleeved Satin Blouse is cleverly stitched to give the effect of a Chemisette. In Green, Blue, Black with White; also Brown with Beige. In three fittings.

6½ GNS.

This tailored Frock with its Short Coat is of RODIER'S Floquella. The Frock has Collar and Cuffs of white Crepe —Colourings include Reseda, Azure Blue, Citron Gazelle, Lacquer Red, Spanish Brown, Navy and Black—flecked with White. In three fittings.

6½ GNS.

5½ GNS.

Three-Piece Frock in fine artificial Crepe Romaine. The short Coatee opens over a tuck-in Blouse, and is cleverly embroidered on shoulders and sleeve. In Black and White ; also Navy and White. In three graduated hip fittings.

5½ GNS.

Day Frock in artificial Crepe Romaine; the original skirt frilled at the back has "almost a bustle." In Black, Navy, Cedar, Madonna Blue—with a White collar. In three graduated hip fittings from Very Small to stock sizes.

Smart upturned hat of fine quality fur felt—cleverly tucked on right side of brim, with bow at back. In Black, Navy, Beige, Grey, Lido, India Red.

39/6

Attractive Toque in felt and Racello straw with bow tied across back in the two materials. In Black, Beige, Navy, Lido and Green.

69/6

FENWICK, LADIES TAILORS, 60-63, NEW BOND STREET, W.

COME TO-DAY TO SEE the lovely and inexpensive clothes being shown

"*But as time passes we find that the clothes of the past do not fit, do not serve us anymore.*"

—*PARDONABLE LIES*

THE CLOTHES
OF THE PAST

I n this passage, Maurice Blanche is not talking about fabric and
thread, though clothing is a useful metaphor. Maisie's mentor is
challenging her thoughts and opinions, decisions made in the past
that no longer fit who she has become and how she lives now. It is
perhaps advice we might all heed, and certainly the passage resonated
with readers who cite it as one of the most cherished pieces of advice
offered by Maurice.

Arguably one of the crucial ways in which we miss an opportunity
to grow is in our opinions, not just of other people or situations, but
also in the view we have of ourselves. The passage was inspired in part
by a conversation I'd had with a friend. I had mentioned someone
we had both known many years ago and how he was now an accom-
plished artist. Before I had even finished speaking, the friend inter-
rupted me, recounting what a "waster" that person had been, how
he had borrowed money from everyone we knew and never paid it
back. Then he began to list a number of infractions committed by the
friend—I thought it would never end. I waited until he had finished

and said, "Yes, but he was only twenty years old then—he's fifty-five now, and who knows what demons he was dealing with?"

Letting go of old opinions—being open to new information about people, situations and ourselves—is at the heart of continuing to grow, even as we age. This is the lesson that Maurice wanted Maisie to understand. Shedding the clothing of the past can release us into a different future, liberating us from the anchors of regret, prejudice and inflexibility. Perhaps, like trees, we can only become green and blossom again when last year's leaves have browned, fallen and been swept away.

How might it be if you looked at your own deeply held opinions and beliefs and turned over each one as if it were a stone with many threads of color and texture? Do those opinions and beliefs still serve you? How would it be if you were open to new information, a fresh approach—and exercised the freedom to change your mind? Write about your excavation here, remembering to let the questions linger, and come back to the task of making notes as and when you have something you want to record.

Original artwork by
Andrew Davidson for
Elegy for Eddie

With an enthusiastic flourish, yards of vibrant purples, yellows, pinks, and reds of Indian silk were pulled out, to be rubbed between finger and thumb, and held against her face in front of the mirror. . . . Thus a day that had seen so many tears ended in the midst of a rainbow.

—MAISIE DOBBS

OUR PERSONAL
BOLTS OF COLOR

This scene is from *Maisie Dobbs*. Maisie had been questioning a young married woman about her former love, a man who had survived the war, but with terrible facial wounds. Maisie is endeavoring to find out more about the circumstances of his death. The woman's grief and lingering melancholy are palpable, and for her part, Maisie knows it is important to leave the woman in a lighter mood, with a positive outlook and some joy in her heart. She takes her to Liberty, the London store famous for its fabric department, where the women look at the new silk fabrics from India. Soon the woman has an assistant pulling out bolts of soft, luscious color—and when she sees the woman's demeanor change, Maisie takes her leave.

We all have our "bad" days—how would we ever know the good, light days if we didn't? But there are also days when, perhaps, we are taken lower by grief or regret, or the sharp, bittersweet memories of someone beloved who is no longer in our life. That is the point when we need the bolts of color: a chance to find some joy in a rainbow. And for each of us that looks a little different.

For me, time spent in nature, whether on the land or simply pulling weeds in my garden, can elevate my spirit on those dark days. When my father was nearing the end of his life, I would return from a day spent at his bedside in the hospice and walk miles across the fields near my parents' rural home. For me, the fabric was every shade of green in the fields and trees around me. Color came to me in watching new lambs at first unsteady on young legs, then, as the days passed, jumping around, growing in strength until they ventured from their mothers to play. On one occasion I helped a farmer return a herd of cattle to their field after they'd managed to break through a fence—I came home flushed with the effort and, in a way, closer to my roots, which are in the country. Nature has always been one of my most effective prescriptions.

So what would your prescription be, if you were your own apothecary? When working with clients in my coaching practice, I would often ask this question: If you had five ingredients that formed your everyday prescription, what would they be? Here are mine: My work—writing. Reading. A good walk, either alone or with a friend, but always with my dog. Riding my horse. Time spent with my partner. I should probably add "eating sensibly," because I do not do well if I resort to snacking or if I eat too many sweet things. I think my brother's day would never be complete if he could not work on one of his classic cars. My husband plays his guitar daily—it's a must. A friend loves to paint and keeps her watercolors out on a tray, so that even though she has a very demanding job, at some point when she gets home, she takes up her brushes and adds color and texture to whatever she's working on. My late mother went straight out to her garden as soon as she arrived home from work; even if she only deadheaded the roses or pulled a few weeds, that was a part of her day, her prescription. For another friend, it's detouring via the florist on the way home from work, even if her purchase is just a simple bunch of daffodils, golden silk for her table.

Invariably we can't hit every ingredient in our daily prescription, but if we can just get to one or two, we can end the day closer to that rainbow the woman experienced in *Maisie Dobbs*, as bolts of color were brought for her to rub between finger and thumb.

If you were to compile your daily prescription of five components, what would they be? How might it be if you committed to achieving one or two each day?

. . . .
. . . .
. . . .
. . . .
. . . .
. . . .
. . . .
. . . .
. . . .
. . . .
. . . .
. . . .
. . . .

The quote on the opposite page was used as an epigraph to introduce a book in the Maisie Dobbs series, and has proved to be a favorite with readers. If it resonates with you, write about it here.

···

···

···

···

···

···

···

···

···

···

···

···

···

···

···

···

···

···

···

···

···

···

···

Once in a while you will stumble upon the truth
but most of us manage to pick ourselves up
and hurry along as if nothing had happened.

—WINSTON CHURCHILL

"*I know you will comport yourself with excellence
in the face of such a change in circumstance.*"

—THE MAPPING OF LOVE AND DEATH

WHEN CIRCUMSTANCES CHANGE

A change in circumstance can come to anyone at any time. Loss of a job, a home, a loved one—and you can add loss of confidence, loss of health. And for some people, those losses just mount up. The character Billy Beale—beloved by readers—is one of those people for whom life seems to be just "one thing after another." Yet Billy soldiers on, making the best of his circumstances. But in this passage, it's Maisie in the spotlight, and her change in circumstance at first blush seems to be so positive, though even great or good change can come with untold challenges—one only has to consider the lottery winners who go on to experience a fractured home life, a loss of community as distrust creeps in or a misplaced sense of self as the gathering of "stuff" takes precedence over nourishment of the soul.

Certainly Maisie is challenged by the legacy she's received, but she learns to temper her knee-jerk attempts to lift others away from their difficulties with her newfound wealth. Her generosity becomes an Achilles' heel, so she is forced to come back to her value of honoring others—especially their ability to elevate themselves up and out of a situation—rather than rushing to offer more than the helping hand of moral support.

This passage was inspired by observing others go through life-changing alterations in circumstance. One friend suffered a dreadful accident, but following a period of grief over the loss of mobility, he forced himself to stop focusing on the list of things he could not do; rather, he looked to the many options still available to him, and there were some he'd never even considered but went on to enjoy. As one door closed, others opened. When writing this piece, I thought of the people who had experienced a change in circumstance, and I realized that those who emerged stronger and wiser were the ones who achieved a conscious awareness of who they were, what they stood for and the breadth of what was available to them in life. Wealth, health and property can all be lost and gained in a finger snap. Who we are in the maelstrom that life can pitch us into, is the person we come home to every time we look into the mirror.

Have you had a change in circumstance? And remember, even the good things can challenge us—a new relationship, a development in an old relationship, a job gained—opportunities we either rush toward or rear away from. How did that change feel? Were you scared? Were you excited? Do you think you remained grounded—and if so, what inner resources came to your aid? If you gained something, did you lose something else along the way? And if the opposite happened and you experienced loss, might you have acquired something in the process? What did you learn about how you might comport yourself in the face of future life changes? What resources do you now know you can draw upon? All big questions—and ones that Maisie has faced time and again. A reminder: Don't rush to answer these questions. Instead allow the questions to linger, to go below the surface, to touch the wisdom you hold inside.

···
···
···
···
···
···
···
···
···
···
···
···
···
···
···
···
···
···
···
···

"I've come to the conclusion that liking a person we are required to have dealings with is not of paramount importance, Maisie. But respect is crucial, on both sides, as is tolerance and a depth of understanding of those influences that sculpt a character."

—MESSENGER OF TRUTH

THE VALUE OF RESPECT

When I was in my early teens, I had a teacher whom I did not like at all. She was strict, never smiled and gave us no quarter if we were caught speaking to a classmate or gazing out the window, even for a second. She had eyes like a hawk, and we referred to her as the "harridan."

I was complaining to my mother about the harridan one day, telling her how much we all disliked the teacher. "That's all very well," she said. "But do you respect her?"

I shrugged in the way that teenage girls are wont to shrug, and I gave the question a little thought. "Well, I suppose so," I said.

"That's all right, then," said my mother. "No one ever said you had to like your teachers—but respect is important."

I thought about this exchange a lot at the time, and I began paying attention not only to that teacher, but to others at the school, and to people beyond the school whom I interacted with—shopkeepers, neighbors, friends and family. I came to understand how respect is earned, and it is a two-way street—and I remember considering another teacher at the school whom everyone liked but in truth few respected. She was younger than most of the teachers, funny, a little bit edgy in her comments, and her classes were somewhat boisterous. But she was always behind with marking our work and it took ages to find out our grades. As a class we began to have mixed feelings, and for some of the girls it came out as insolence or missed homework—what was the point if you didn't get your work back? I found myself daydreaming in her classes, staring out the window and writing stories in my head, and at the end of the year I knew I hadn't really earned my A grade. I'd coasted by on a few classroom laughs and a wave of inertia.

Examples from life aren't always so clear-cut, but those experiences gave me food for thought. In later years I thought about that strict teacher. I'd done well in her class because she held our feet to the fire, and every minute in her company was time spent doing what we were supposed to be doing—learning. She came to mind many times when I was training to be a teacher, when I considered the challenges that came with responsibility for imparting a dense academic subject and inculcating a sense of personal dignity into the lives of girls in their early teens, for with that dignity came a desire to do well.

Years later the question of respect came up again, when I worked for what was considered to be a very high-powered company in London. On my first day, one of my new coworkers described the CEO to me: "He's not what you'd call a people person—not very likable at all—but everyone around here respects him." I discovered that he was as described—not very likable, not at first, anyway—but he was fair, and he knew every single job at the firm because he'd worked his way up and hence demanded the very best of everyone who worked there. And in time, as I settled into the job and grew to know my way around, I found him to be quite good company. I realized he was a person with a great deal of responsibility, and not only for the success of the business. I believe he understood his responsibility to the people he hired, to ensure the security of their jobs, which in turn meant their financial security and job satisfaction.

In this passage regarding respect, Maurice is speaking of empathy and suggesting that, before we rush to declare whether we like a person, perhaps there's wisdom in considering who that person is, along with an insight into his or her life. In the same way, we might consider our part in ensuring that points of contact are positive and our role in finding paths to mutual respect. Often, when those aspects of relationships are subject to some effort, we discover that a level of affection is not such a leap after all.

Have you had an experience of respecting someone who you perhaps did not really like—or a person you liked, but for whom you felt little respect? Write about it here, adding any new insights time might have offered you.

. . . .

. . . .

. . . .

. . . .

. . . .

. . . .

. . . .

. . . .

. . . .

She was not in the mood for Robert MacFarlane's games.
After all, Maisie Dobbs was her father's daughter,
and any sort of manipulation did not sit well with her.

—A LESSON IN SECRETS

MANIPULATION
AND VALUES

found it interesting to note how many readers have written to me about this passage—hence its inclusion in the book. In this passage, Maisie Dobbs feels she is being manipulated by Robert MacFarlane, a character who has always presented her with something of a dilemma, though there is a suggestion that they both enjoy the snappy banter that passes between them. To be fair, Maisie tires of it sooner than MacFarlane.

As someone who has been encouraged to "know thyself," Maisie is fully aware of those times when she is being manipulated. She knows when someone is trying to bend her thoughts and actions against her will. Sometimes she falls into the trap—no human being is perfect—but most of the time she is alert to any attempt to maneuver her in an unattractive direction. Why is she "her father's daughter"? Because Frankie Dobbs is a very down-to-earth man, one who will speak his mind and not be pushed away from his dearly held values and ethics.

The question "What would Maisie do?" must be considered in light of her self-knowledge. Her meditation practice, her soul-searching and her self-reflection all serve to underpin her decision not to be swayed to do something unless she sees benefit in it—and in her case the benefit is usually in service to another person or to her country. But what can we take from Maisie's stand? Perhaps this is where a little self-examination will give us the benchmarks for dealing with attempts to manipulate us and ultimately give us the ability to say no when it serves us to do so.

Quite simply, what values do you live by? If you could list five core values that form the foundation of your life, what would they be? This exercise is not as easy as it sounds, because once established, those values will rise up and have bearing on every decision you make and give weight when you answer yes or no to a request.

When I tasked myself with identifying my core values, I realized I had to be clear and distinct—it was no good waffling around the words (this might be the time to reflect upon your response to "On the Power of Distinction"). My values seemed to be steeped in words such as "truth," "honesty," "integrity," "honor," "balance." All very nice, but what would they mean in real life? Where was truth when that little white lie seemed to be the more attractive and more comfortable option? I gave a great deal of thought to the word "truth"—and that's probably why it comes up so often in the Maisie Dobbs series. It's crucial for an investigator to dig deep for the truth of a matter, and on a personal level, excavating to reveal our truth is a quest for a nugget worth pursuing. I had to ask what "integrity" meant to me—what were its boundaries? I gave myself situations to consider and did the same for the other words I'd listed. Time and again the importance of distinction seemed paramount—and a deep level of personal confession.

What are the values you live by? How do you think Maisie Dobbs might counsel you to consider the question? If honesty is a value, give yourself examples of how you have demonstrated honesty and consider the occasions when you felt the greatest challenge in honoring the value. Have you ever crossed your own code of ethics to manipulate someone else? Have you manipulated your core values to avoid conflict or to find the easy way out of a problem? How did that feel? Be honest. Any manipulation of our values by our own actions will not sit well with us—in the same way that manipulation by Robert MacFarlane does not sit well with Maisie Dobbs!

....
....
....
....
....
....
....
....
....
....
....
....
....
....

ON LOCATION

Kent

When I wrote *An Incomplete Revenge*, the fifth book in the Maisie Dobbs series, one of my friends commented, "This book is your love letter to Kent." And yes, upon reflection, I believe it was, though the county of Kent appears in each of the novels. Whenever Maisie ventures from London to Kent and the fictional village of Chelstone, she is in my home county, and in my mind's eye, I am right there with her.

I love the Weald of Kent—the word "weald" is derived from the old Anglo-Saxon "wald," meaning "forest." Over the centuries much of the legendary forest that covered the county has been lost to development, but acres upon acres remain, with great tracts of woodland spread out across the land. If you took me into the woodland of Kent blindfolded, I would know I was home simply by the fragrance in the air, a certain feel to the breeze and the sounds of the birds. My first home was a tied cottage—"tied" to the land and to my father's job on a farm some two miles from Goudhurst, a small village set amid the farms and forests that are a hallmark of the area. The Kent I wanted to bring to my readers was the Kent of undulating countryside, where hops, barley, apples, pears, blackcurrants, cherries and strawberries flourished. I wanted to set Maisie Dobbs in the Kent of wild garlic and celandines growing in abundance alongside freshwater streams meandering through deep woodland. I wanted readers to see the Kent of wildflowers flourishing on grassy verges; of bluebells carpeting forests of beech, hornbeam and chestnut; of primroses and white anemones, those subtle smudges of color, amid the moss under an oak tree. And I wanted you, the reader, to see the hop-picking season as it was before the war, and oast houses with their cowls poking up like witches' hats in the morning mist.

Kent becomes an important part of Maisie's life when she is sent to be a companion and maid to Lord Julian Compton's dowager mother. The quiet calm of Chelstone Manor, the ancestral country home of the Compton family, provides Maisie with the solitude she needs to study. She is a London girl who comes to love the country. Longtime readers will know the significance of the Dower House, the traditional home of the widow of the lord of the manor, which is sold to her mentor, Dr. Maurice Blanche, after the dowager dies.

Though the village of Chelstone is a fiction, along with Chelstone Manor, I can see both the location and architecture in my mind's eye.

I envisage Chelstone to be just north of Pembury in Kent and due south of Tonbridge—you can look up those places online or on a map of Kent. Chelstone has a branch-line station that joins the main line at Tonbridge, which makes it easy for Maisie to travel into London.

I have imagined the house to look something like Pashley Manor, near the village of Ticehurst in East Sussex, which is close to the county's boundary with Kent. I have visited Pashley Manor many times over the years; indeed, it's a favorite destination when guests come to stay with me during my sojourns in England. The front aspect of the house was built in 1550, yet a large extension was added on to the back in Georgian times. I have imagined Chelstone to have similar architecture, but the other way around, with the Georgian part of the house at the front and the beamed sixteenth-century wing behind it, looking out over the grounds. The Pashley Manor Gardens are a delight, and the manor is surrounded by fields and farms, just as I have imagined Chelstone Manor in its rural setting.

As the Maisie Dobbs series moves in time from the years of the Great War to the Second World War, so the county of Kent plays its part. During the Great War, those who lived near or visited the coasts of Kent and Sussex could hear the cannonade on the other side of the English Channel, and it was in the skies above Kent's peaceful countryside that the Battle of Britain raged.

The quote on the opposite page was used as an epigraph to introduce a book in the Maisie Dobbs series, and has proved to be a favorite with readers. If it resonates with you, write about it here.

❧

....
....
....
....
....
....
....
....
....
....
....
....
....
....
....
....
....
....
....
....
....
....

You shall leave everything loved most dearly, and this is the shaft of which the bow of exile shoots first. You shall prove how salt is the taste of another man's bread and how hard is the way up and down another man's stairs.

—DANTE, *PARADISO*

*She would not allow someone for whom
she had so little regard to have a negative effect
on her mood at the start of a new week.*

—PARDONABLE LIES

EXTINGUISHING NEGATIVE POWER

Again we come to the question of how we view others and their power over us. In this scene, Maisie knows the tone and approach of another person could have a negative effect on her, but she understands she has a choice in how she responds to and absorbs the other person's "energy." She can protect and retain her own positive mood, or she can allow the action or reaction of another person to bring her down in some way. This is something we all face at one point or another: We're in a good frame of mind, positive about our day or week, or a project we're engaged in, and then *wham!* Along comes another person with one simple comment that bursts our bubble, and it changes our energy, our attitude, even how *we* approach others—perhaps that negative comment has become a virus, and not only have we caught it, but we're spreading it!

When I first worked in academic publishing, it was my job to visit universities and talk to professors about our books and try to find a fit between our products and their courses. I enjoyed my work, and even though it required cold-calling and was sometimes a bit of a slog, I knew a sunny disposition would always get me an invitation to discuss the courses and our books—and as I was also responsible for product development, like any salesperson I understood that good relationships led to greater success. I remember calling on a professor I knew, and as I entered his office, he looked up, greeted me and seemed to study my ears. "Did you know it's unlucky to wear moonstone?" he said. I reached up to touch one of my lovely new moonstone earrings, a gift from a dear friend. I brushed off the comment with a laugh, and we began the meeting. As soon as I left the professor's office, I took off the earrings—and worried all day about the bad luck that was going to befall me. I did my best to shake off the energy that seemed to envelop me the second this prediction of bad luck came my way. I remember telling my mother about the professor and his belief that moonstone was unlucky, and she said, "What a load of nonsense—a stone doesn't bring bad luck." I thought that was pretty rich from someone who was so superstitious, she wouldn't pass another person on the stairs, but that comment was worthy of thought. I had given my energy to another person's belief, and it had impacted my day.

So how do we maintain the very best of ourselves when we encounter a wall of negativity? What would Maisie do?

Before anything else, Maisie would pay attention to her posture. People often underestimate the importance and impact of posture, but if we stand tall and strong in the face of criticism, it is as if we are giving strength to our personal moral code and our sense of self. In allowing our body to demonstrate its strength, we are holding up a hand and saying, "Stop!" We're also saying "Stop!" to that voice within, the one that might agree with the assailant and begin to diminish our self-confidence. The fact that I kept touching the offending earring during my meeting meant that my attention was not fully on my work or even on protecting myself from the most dangerous thing in the room, which was the energy in that comment. When I look back, I know I might well have started to slump!

Maisie would also take action, deciding to do something positive to bring in light rather than support darkness. As noted in "Our Personal Bolts of Color," in *Maisie Dobbs* she changes the outlook of a young woman who has been diminished by her circumstances by taking her into a shop to look at new fabrics, ensuring that a day attended with so much darkness ends with a memory of vibrant colors.

There are two other factors to consider—ones that no doubt Maisie would have brought to mind. The first is the contradiction inherent in the apparent negative comment or event. She might ask the question, "Is there something I should pay attention to here?" If there is legitimate criticism, perhaps there is room at some point to look hard at the grain of truth, accepting that it might contribute to personal growth. The second and arguably most important thing to remember is that any opinion about a subject belongs to the person holding the opinion—and we sometimes forget this. It reflects so much about that person, and not just his or her likes and dislikes. Any expression of opinion might reveal education, culture, breadth of knowledge and ability to communicate. Thus any negative opinion should never be allowed to change your mood—it belongs to someone else, after all.

In the face of a negative encounter, Maisie would stand tall and endeavor to go forward into her day with a light step. Can you remember a time when you have felt your power ebb in the face of negativity? Or perhaps another occasion when you stood firm in the face of a comment that might otherwise have wounded you? Write about it here, and note the steps you would like to remember, the empowering actions and thoughts you would like to draw upon should such an occasion arise again.

_____

_____
_____
_____
_____
_____
_____
_____
_____
_____
_____
_____
_____
_____
_____
_____
_____
_____
_____
_____
_____

"I'll tell you this. Leaving that which you love breaks your heart open. But you will find a jewel inside, and this precious jewel is the opening of your heart to all that is new and all that is different, and it will be the making of you— if you allow it to be."

—LEAVING EVERYTHING MOST LOVED

THE MYSTERY
OF DEPARTURE

M aisie Dobbs receives this advice from an Indian woman whom she has visited during the course of an investigation, to gain more insight into the circumstances regarding the death of a young woman originally from India who had been living and working in London. Now Maisie has her own plans to leave home—to learn something more of herself, of the world—and in so doing, she hopes to gain a measure of insight, of wisdom to carry her forward into the future.

The passage was inspired by not only my own experiences as an immigrant in another country, but the fact that I come from a country with a deep history of immigration and now live in a country that also can attribute much of its "melting pot" history and growth to immigrants from other lands. Over the years I have had many opportunities to speak to people about their experiences of leaving home, leaving family and friends to seek out the new, and I have witnessed the bittersweet moment of reflection upon the life left behind, memories mirrored by the opportunities—and challenges—inherent in arrival at a new place. Yet we do not have to leave a country to experience that breaking open of the heart, that pulling apart of the shell. We might simply move to another house, another job, or we might be leaving a situation or a certain time of life. The grief that attends losing someone close to us also heralds a leaving, as we move into a future without them.

The passage underlines the fact that the discomfort of farewell cannot be avoided, yet as in a tunnel, there is a pinprick of light at the end—and in moving toward that light we can grasp the opportunity to learn more about ourselves as we garner the qualities of endurance, resilience and compassion required for the journey of assimilation. And as is often the case, we do not recognize the growth inherent in the experience of leaving until we return.

No matter what the journey is that requires us to leave the known and comfortable, as the character Lakshmi Chaudary Jones says, "The mystery of departure awaits."

Reflect upon a time when you have had to leave everything most loved. For some it is the moment they left their parents' home or graduated from college. This has been one of the most repeated quotes from the Maisie Dobbs series of novels—everyone, it seems, has experienced the mystery of departure.

* * *

. . . .

. . . .

. . . .

. . . .

"And you think journeying abroad
will give you this knowledge you crave?"

"I think it will contribute to my understanding
of the world, of people."

"More so than, say, the old lady who has lived in the same
house her entire life, who has borne children both alive and
dead? Who tends her soil; who sees the sun shine and the
rain fall over the land, winter, spring, summer, and autumn?
What might you say to the idea that we all have a capacity for
wisdom, just as a jug has room for a finite amount of water—
pouring more water in the jug doesn't increase that capacity."

—LEAVING EVERYTHING MOST LOVED

THE WISDOM OF
REMAINING IN PLACE

I remember reading that for every statement of what is so, there is a contradiction. In this passage, one of my favorite characters, the Benedictine nun Dame Constance Charteris, challenges Maisie's plans to travel overseas.

This scene was inspired by observations I made in childhood, living in rural Kent, England. Much of my time—especially during school breaks—was spent on local farms, where my mother worked until I was about eleven years of age, and where I worked during school breaks until I left to go to college. Given the proximity of these farms, many of the local residents in our hamlet were agricultural workers living in tied accommodation—that's housing "tied" to a job and the land. As a community, our year revolved around the seasons—from preparing the fields and hop gardens in winter and spring, to picking strawberries and blackcurrants in midsummer, to harvesting the grain in high summer and the apples and pears that followed, often at the same time hops were ready to be picked. I learned early that for everything there was a season. And I remember once commenting to my mother that some of the older members of our community seemed to know everything—yet they'd never lived anywhere else and never traveled, except perhaps for a day at the beach in Hastings. That was when my mother told me that you didn't necessarily have to be a world traveler to learn about life—not when you were so close to nature and saw into the heart of birth, life and death every single day.

It's certainly food for thought. As I grew older I came to learn that most of those seniors had in one way or another traveled to another world—a land of war, of peace or of the unknown—as the years advanced with the breadth of innovation every decade of the twentieth century left in its wake. It could be argued that we leave everything most loved with each new experience that demands we grow.

What have you learned from the elders in your community or your family, especially as you embarked upon your journey into the wider world—even if that wider world was only a few miles away? Remember: Not all journeys require physical distance. Give yourself time to ponder this question—and if you are of an age when you have yet to spend significant time with your elders, make time for some interesting conversations. Ask questions. Listen with the ear of your heart.

* * *

. . . .

. . . .

. . . .

. . . .

. . . .

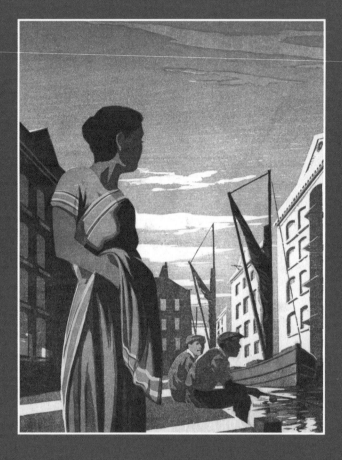

Original artwork by
Andrew Davidson for
Leaving Everything Most Loved

I have learned that if you must leave a place that you have lived in and loved and where all your yesteryears are buried deep—leave it any way except a slow way, leave it the fastest way you can.

—BERYL MARKHAM, *WEST WITH THE NIGHT*

"*Maisie, we have our freedom, both of us.*
We are lucky, very lucky. Make sure you use it well."

—JOURNEY TO MUNICH

USING FREEDOM WISELY

The notion that freedom is something to be cherished, something to "use well," is not new and has resonated throughout time. In the 1960s, the British singer-songwriter Donovan crafted the lyrics, "Freedom is a word I rarely use without thinking." Coincidentally, another war was being fought at the time and another generation of young men lost to conflict. But there is so much more to the warning given by the character Leon Donat to Maisie. They have both seen freedom wrenched from the people of Munich—the freedom to speak without dreading retribution, to have confidence in a free press, and to walk the streets without fear. And the freedom to live without fear is arguably the most crucial on a personal and collective level.

Maisie is being counseled to use her freedom wisely—with the most important word being "use." It is the sort of advice Maisie would take to heart, would mull over to establish what it might mean in her life, to live to the very bounds of her freedom—but wisely. It is advice she will come back to time and again, exercising her freedom to work independently, to choose how and where she lives and, ultimately, to gather into her circle those she loves—and even her right to bring new loves into her life.

This passage was inspired by personal experience, though perhaps not as colorful as Maisie's. It was advice given to me many years ago when my dog—an enormous, beautiful and beloved blue Great Dane—died while undergoing surgery. I had passed on opportunities to travel, to spread my wings and take up a new job in another country, all because I had a very big dog who wasn't in the best of health. Then he died, and I was grief-stricken. A friend called to offer me solace, and at the end of our conversation he said, "He's given you your freedom. Use it wisely." I took his words to heart, and I decided to come to the United States on a "sabbatical." Almost as soon as I landed, one opportunity led to another—not that anything was easy; at times it was far from it—and on each occasion I remembered that beautiful Great Dane, and I reminded myself that I had my precious freedom to choose what I might do next. At the time of writing these words, that was almost twenty-eight years ago.

I came to believe that one of the most important acts of self-inquiry is to try to express thoughts and feelings about freedom. What does the word "freedom" mean to you? At a time when, according to the United Nations High Commissioner for Refugees, there are some 68.5 million displaced people in camps across the globe, it might seem somewhat indulgent, but I believe that is exactly why we have to consider it, because we must claim every freedom we can. Sometimes claiming freedom might be very simple—time alone to read, the purchase of a bouquet of flowers on a Friday to enjoy over the weekend. Those would be massive freedoms for people living amid terror and squalor. So perhaps exercising our freedom is to use our voice—

committing to using our freedom of expression on behalf of those who do not have such an advantage, whether in our community, our country or internationally. It's up to us how we use our freedom—which is a freedom in itself. And writing about freedom and what it means to us is liberating. Try it here. Commit to the words of Donovan and never use the word without thinking.

....
....
....
....
....
....
....
....
....
....
....
....
....
....
....
....
....
....
....
....
....
....
....

*Maisie knew only too well that
the path of grief could not be scripted.*

—AMONG THE MAD

*"Grief is not an event, my dear, but a passage,
a pilgrimage along a path that allows us to reflect upon
the past from points of remembrance held in the soul.
At times the way is filled with stones underfoot and
we feel pained by our memories, yet on other days the
shadows reflect our longing and those happinesses shared."*

—MESSENGER OF TRUTH

THE PATH OF GRIEF

Passages concerning grief in the Maisie Dobbs novels have been quoted back to me many times by readers—possibly because we have all experienced grief and have been faced with navigating our way through a time that is so very different for everyone. I think anyone who has lost a loved one has come across a sense of expectation that they should be "over it" or "moving on" from the grief at a certain point. Perhaps after a year or two years there is an expectation that we will be past the pain.

Certainly, time heals the initial deep wounds of grief, but that time is different for everyone, and how we mourn a loss is a passage belonging only to the person bereaved. And we know that intense feelings of grief can attend loss of a job, an opportunity, a beloved pet or a way of life.

I've often thought the age-old tradition of wearing black for a year following a bereavement wasn't such a bad idea. The weeds of mourning told everyone that you were in a place of deep sadness, that a door had closed and the new one was not yet open. Your drawn curtains said, "I am not ready for your world yet." When the first anniversary of the loss had passed, it was tradition to wear lavender for as long as you needed. The color informed people that you were ready to move into the light again, that you were taking small steps into the world of color, of endeavor, and gently taking your place in the community once more. One day you would emerge from your cocoon of safety wearing clothes from the time before the loss of someone held dear, someone you loved. You would have passed through the passage of grief.

I am sure there were cases where the bereaved were encouraged to "get out there" in those earlier days, but at the same time, there was a certain reverence for the individual, a deep heartfelt emotion.

I have received many email messages about these excerpts, and about Maisie's own passage through grief, leading me to believe the resonance might be due to experiences of being pushed too soon into bringing the journey of bereavement to a speedy close so that others do not have to experience discomfort when faced with one who is grief-stricken. Loss is not a virus, but not all are at ease among those in mourning. I have learned by experience that it is important to honor one's own voice, one's own needs, especially during difficult times. Yes, we have to engage with our family, and work and other responsibilities cannot be set aside for long, but claiming time each day to be with our thoughts and feelings, and over whatever period it takes to be at peace, is an important gift to the self.

Have you experienced a loss? What supported you during those dark times of mourning? What wisdom can you bring from your own experience as an offering of support to others you might encounter who are in the midst of enduring a bereavement?

Leicester Square underground station in the mid-1930s.
When I first saw Maisie Dobbs in my mind's eye,
she was making her way up the old escalator at
Warren Street Station, and it looked something like this.
I knew the station in the 1970s, when I worked for
a company located in Fitzroy Square.

"*Truth has a certain buoyancy—*
it makes its way to the surface, in time."

—IN THIS GRAVE HOUR

TRUTH'S BUOYANCY

"Truth"—the word comes up time and again in the Maisie Dobbs novels. It is at the heart of Maisie's work as she delves deep to discover the truth about an event, a person and, indeed, herself.

As a writer of fiction, it is also part of my remit to dig for the truth, to create layers of questions leading to that holy grail, truth. The writer Khaled Hosseini said, "Writing fiction is the act of weaving a series of lies to arrive at a greater truth."

The quotes about truth in the Maisie Dobbs series have been voiced back to me time and again by those readers who keep a log of "advice" spoken by Maisie, Maurice Blanche or one of the other characters during the course of a story. Perhaps it's because, in one way or another, truth is crucial to human beings living in community with one another. Even to those who live a lie, the truth is important, lest it be uncovered and they are revealed to be imposters—and there are many kinds of imposters in this world. However, those passages were, like so many in my writing, inspired by observations—the very same observations those of us who read the news and pay attention might arrive at. Truth does come out eventually—we've all read articles that attest to its buoyancy. Perhaps that truth might take centuries to bob to the surface or it might take a week, but I would not want to be in the shoes of the liar, whether the person is a public figure—perhaps a politician or a celebrity lying about an affair, or the leader of a corporation misleading the public—or an individual who claims not to have witnessed a crime when it was clear he or she was the only witness. Truth rises to the surface given time—let us consider the connection between tobacco and lung cancer, or the link between plastics and high toxicity levels in our oceans. Lies are falsehoods, and as Maisie knows, a lie cannot be shackled; truth will undo the bounds of even the most innocuous fib.

None of us is without blame, and sometimes truth is withheld to protect people, and that's always a difficult path, because we risk offending those loved ones we are trying to shield perhaps they want to meet the truth head-on. I think we all understand that the truths Maurice speaks and the truth Maisie searches for in her work are not the truths we suppress to protect others.

What does it mean to you to live by the truth? It's a big question and means something different to everyone.

"Maurice."

"Yes?"

*"I have loved you as if you were my father,
though that has never stopped me loving my father."*

"I know. And you are as my daughter."

—THE MAPPING OF LOVE AND DEATH

LOVE AND FAMILY

I n this passage, Maisie acknowledges the depth of her love and regard for her mentor, Maurice Blanche, as he is dying. They speak to each other as father and daughter, yet there is never a doubt as to the depth of the enduring love she has for her father, Frankie Dobbs. Maurice has been father to Maisie's intellectual and professional growth. He has helped her use her innate gifts of intuition and insight to forge a life and purpose she might not have imagined as a girl growing up in Lambeth, a poor area of London.

The passage was inspired by the knowledge that for many of us there are people in our lives who have played a part akin to parents, though they could never have taken the place of the parents we love. There could be the family friend who has become a mentor, or a teacher at school who has taken you under her wing, or the employer who identifies a competence you were not aware of, yet once noted and encouraged, it enables you to shine. There is comfort in having such people in our lives, if we are so fortunate.

On a personal note, the relationship between Maisie and Maurice was not inspired by any one person, but an amalgam of individuals known in childhood and the years of my growing: There was the teacher who encouraged me to read widely, another teacher who pressed me to keep writing when "composition" was seen as the easy choice in English classes. There was the employer who saw my enthusiasm for my work and gave me new opportunities, and another who made sure my new ideas went "up the ladder," paving the way for promotion. All were mentors, and each in their way combined to guide me through life experiences that were outside my parents' frame of reference. That Frankie Dobbs not only understands his daughter's bond with Maurice, but holds her mentor in high esteem for his part in her life, is inspired by my father's love and support as he encouraged me to find my own path. Like Maisie, I had only one beloved father—but also a respected few mentors who held my hand along the way.

Have you been fortunate enough to have mentors on your life's journey? If you were to write a letter of gratitude, what would you say?

. . . .

. . . .

. . . .

. . . .

. . . .

. . . .

. . . .

. . . .

Original artwork by
Andrew Davidson
for *An Incomplete Revenge*

Maisie stepped away from the house, but before setting off in the direction of the underground station, she looked back and considered the many houses that seemed so ordinary on the outside—yet inside their shells lingered untold human sadness. "May they know peace," she whispered, and went on her way.

—IN THIS GRAVE HOUR

YOUR HOUSE OF PEACE

T he inspiration for this passage has its roots in the experience
described in an earlier section, when I was working in the UK
as an academic representative for a textbook company. My
job involved visiting universities, meeting with professors to discuss
our new books and also to "scout" prospective authors. My specializa-
tion was in technical fields—computer science, engineering, physics,
mathematics—all pretty dry subjects, but I loved my work. The down-
side was the travel. I was twenty-four years of age at the time, and would
leave home on a Sunday and not return until Friday evening; "home"
became the hotels I stayed in from one city to another. It could be
lonely work, because the only people I spoke to during the course of
the week were strangers. In the evenings I would finish work, return
to my hotel for a bite to eat, then go for a walk, often venturing into
residential neighborhoods. As I passed houses with their lights on,
there was something warming about seeing people come home from
work, children sitting down to their homework or a family watching
TV together. It seemed to me that so much of human life could be
experienced during a walk around a neighborhood. One evening I
saw a woman crying as she stood by a window, a telephone receiver

held to her ear. I went on my way, a witness to her grief. Another time I saw a man arguing with his grown son, raising his hand to the boy, who ran from the room. The scene lasted for only the few seconds it took me to pass the house. So many times I saw people enduring some sort of distress, or laughing or arguing together, or simply talking at the dinner table—almost every emotion in life came into focus. Writers tend to squirrel away these experiences, only to bring them out in a story, often decades later.

Inside every home there is a story of joy, of happiness, but equally so there is grief, sadness, disappointment. That is the passage of life and what makes us human. I remember thinking, even then, that I could only wish people peace in the face of those experiences that make our hearts ache, only wish them peace in their homes.

What brings peace to your day? It's not the first time the question has been asked in this book, but sometimes an alternative framing of the question inspires a different answer. Sit with the question of peace in your day, and write your thoughts here, as and when they come to you.

She realized that, in his letters over the years, in his teachings, and in the many pages she would read in the days, weeks, months, and years to come, Maurice would continue to be her guide as she negotiated new terrain. He would not be lost to her forever, and in his own way he had left her with a compass, octant, waywiser, and theodolite, the tools she would need to face a new horizon.

—THE MAPPING OF LOVE AND DEATH

MAPPING YOUR WAY FORWARD

R eaders have often asked me, "Which is your favorite Maisie Dobbs book?" As the creator of the series, that's a tough question—rather like asking a mother to name her favorite child. The first book in the series, *Maisie Dobbs*, has a special place in my heart; I will never forget opening that package, tears streaming across my cheeks as I felt my first published book in my hands. Then came *Birds of a Feather*, inspired by a lesson taught in primary school by my favorite teacher, who became a dear friend. And so it goes on. Each book has its place, and at the heart of each story is a personal connection held dear. However, *The Mapping of Love and Death* holds a very special significance for me, perhaps because the roots of the novel were set firmly in California, where I live now, yet the story unfolded in England, where my own roots run deep. My research took me into the world of maps and mapmakers, into the realm of land surveying and exploration; writers tend to research well beyond what might be required to tell a story, trusting that everything they've learned will inform each word.

As I wrote, I could see so clearly how the process of mapping might be reflected in life's journey and how the presence of a map—a "plan"—facilitated greater exploration; after all, if you are holding a map in your hands, venturing off the beaten track might feel safer, knowing there is a designated route to return to. In the same way, the mapmaker's tools can be seen as a metaphor for qualities that stand us in good stead as we navigate our way forward in life. Maurice has given Maisie her compass, waywiser, octant and theodolite; he has mentored her to a place where she knows the values that will underpin her every decision. He has acknowledged her qualities of perseverance and endurance, and he has recognized her strengths, entrusting her with his legacy.

Values. Perseverance. Endurance. Confidence.

When we have these qualities, negotiating our way through any of life's terrain can be made easier. Perhaps not *easy*—but *easier*. The question is, again, what are your core values? As before, it might seem an easy question, and we can rattle off words such as "integrity," "compassion," "respect"—but what do those words mean in real terms? If we can begin to establish, define and honor our values, even the most daunting of life's challenges can be rendered less worrisome.

You have already been asked to consider the question of values as you worked your way through this book, but it is a topic worthy of reflection and honing, taking into account thoughts, reflections and feelings you might have encountered as you have considered each section. Consider again those five values that will support you as your life unfolds—and life is always unfolding, no matter what your age. What would they be? Look upon them as meaningful as stars in the night sky to a sailor, guiding you in every decision as you chart a course through calm seas or a strong surge of waves topped with white-caps. Maurice challenged Maisie to consider her words with care—to remember the importance of distinctions in language—so when you look at your list, consider what each value means in real terms. Underline your values with every action, for they are your commitments to your deepest self—your compass, in every sense of the word.

⚜

....

....

....

....

....

....

....

....

....

....

....

....

....

....

....

....

....

....

Original artwork by
Andrew Davidson
for *Messenger of Truth*

The quote on the opposite page was used as an epigraph to introduce a book in the Maisie Dobbs series, and has proved to be a favorite with readers. If it resonates with you, write about it here.

....
....
....
....
....
....
....
....
....
....
....
....
....
....
....
....
....
....
....
....
....

If you reveal your secrets to the wind
you should not blame the wind
for revealing them to the trees.

—KAHLIL GIBRAN

"In visiting places and people pertinent to the case, she was honoring her teacher's practice of a 'full accounting' so that work could move on with renewed energy and understanding."

—BIRDS OF A FEATHER

THE FINAL ACCOUNTING

Over the years, many readers of the Maisie Dobbs series have asked me about Maisie's process of her "final accounting." In some books she refers to it as a "personal accounting," though it amounts to the same thing. This is not a financial summing-up, although it often involves presentation of a final bill to be settled. Instead, it's a process whereby Maisie revisits, where possible and as appropriate, the people and places that have been most significant during her work on a case. It is a pilgrimage back into the heart of her investigation, as if she were walking along a corridor, looking into each room as she passes, before closing the door. In going through this accounting process, Maisie is coming to what we might today call "closure": in leaving behind the energy attached to each case, she is able to move on to the next assignment with a clean slate.

This aspect of each novel was inspired by two elements. The first, quite simply, was my own desire as both a reader and a storyteller to have some knowledge of what has come to pass. In a way, I want to see everyone settled again. If mystery is the archetypal journey through chaos to resolution, then I want to see as much of that resolution as

I can—though that isn't always possible, especially with a series that is as much a family saga as a collection of mysteries.

The second element that inspired Maisie's accounting process was my decision to spend time in another country. When I came to the United States, I had no idea I would stay for so long and become settled, though I had intended an extended sabbatical. Before I left my home in the UK, I visited many places of significance in my life. I went back to the place where I was born, the town where I started primary school, and I visited the secondary schools and college I attended. I met up with old friends, drove past the place where I'd had a serious car accident a couple of years earlier—if nothing else, to prove that I could drive along that road again. My sabbatical traveling around the United States was intended to be a time of renewal, so in revisiting people and places of importance in my life, I felt I was preparing the ground for a new season.

When I wrote *Maisie Dobbs,* inclusion of some form of "final accounting" seemed an obvious next step for the character as the story drew to a close. I didn't have to plan or think about it as an idea; it came as part of an organic process of crafting the story. Reflection and intention lead to renewal for Maisie Dobbs.

Readers have shared stories with me of employing a personal accounting in their own lives, especially following life-altering events: a change of job, moving house, divorce, marriage and bereavement. Those are all events that ask us to compile an inventory—a taking stock of who we are and where we are at that point in our lives. The accounting also asks who we might become in the years ahead.

What has Maisie's final accounting meant to you?

Original artwork by
Andrew Davidson
for *Pardonable Lies*

There is a great deal of unmapped
country within us which would have to be
taken into account in an explanation
of our gusts and storms.

—GEORGE ELIOT, *DANIEL DERONDA*

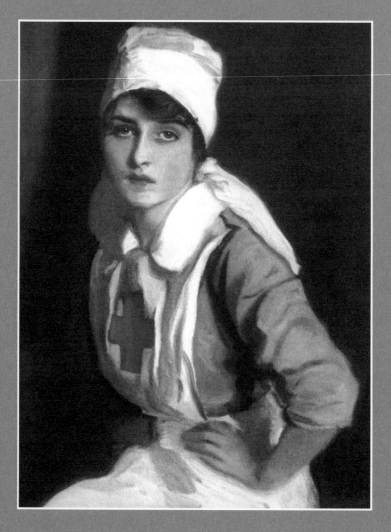

I first saw this image at the
Lost Art of Nursing Museum in
Cannon Beach, Oregon. I immediately
knew that this was how Maisie Dobbs
would have looked during her nursing
service in the Great War.

Additional journaling pages for you to add more quotes from the Maisie Dobbs series.

··
··
··
··
··
··
··
··
··
··
··
··
··
··
··
··
··
··
··
··
··
··
··
··
··

....
....
....
....
....
....
....
....
....
....
....
....
....
....
....
....
....
....
....
....
....
....
....

ACKNOWLEDGMENTS

Whenever a book is created, there is a starting point. An alchemy takes place and the weight of inspiration becomes so heavy that the desire to write that book cannot be ignored—the subject will not be silenced. That's how it was with *Maisie Dobbs*, and every subsequent novel in the series—and that's how it was with *What Would Maisie Do?* As I've explained in the introduction, with each new novel more readers were writing to me quoting favorite passages, asking if I would ever compile a book of "Maurice's wisdom" or "Maisie's words." Then came a tipping point—the something that inspired me to get to grips with the project, and to make it not only a collection of passages from the novels, but an insight into the inspiration underpinning readers' most beloved excerpts. I wanted it to be colorful, to be inspiring, and to be a living document for the reader. Sadly, the tipping point was the passing of one of the most creative people I knew of but never had the pleasure of meeting—Amy Krouse Rosenthal. Amy and I shared the same literary agent—Amy Rennert—and the three of us also shared the same star sign, with birthdays several days apart. I had read Amy Krouse Rosenthal's books; full of life, of curiosity and color, and her video initiative "The Beckoning of Lovely"—in which she challenged people to make things—struck a chord with me. When she died in early 2017, I was at once filled with a desire to do her bidding, which was to get to grips with some of my own beckoning of lovely. I wanted to create something different with the words from my novels, so I turned to the idea that readers had been pressing me to do something about for a while. I began to create *What Would Maisie Do?* I really wish I could tell her how she inspired this book. You challenged people to make things, Amy—so I made this book (of course with help from the really talented people mentioned below). Thank you, dear Amy. So many times, thank you.

My first step was to create a mock-up of *What Would Maisie Do?* which I sent to my agent, Amy Rennert, and with bated breath awaited a response. Amy loved the idea, and passed it on to my long-time editor, Jennifer Barth, who immediately supported the project. With my hand on my heart, much gratitude to you both for your enthusiasm. Sarah Ried, Assistant Editor, has done much of the heavy lifting, along with Dori Carlson and Dani Segelbaum of Harper Design—you did something absolutely wonderful with my amateurish little mock-up and I cannot thank you enough.

Thanks must go to the sources for images used throughout the book, especially Kate Wilson of Pashley Manor in East Sussex, UK, and the staff at the Museum of London's photographic archive, who were particularly helpful. And I am filled with gratitude and admiration for Andrew Davidson, who creates a stunning, iconic image for each new novel in the Maisie Dobbs series, and whose work can be seen throughout *What Would Maisie Do?*

And finally, to the readers and followers of the Maisie Dobbs series, to whom I dedicate *What Would Maisie Do?*—thank you so very much for continuing to inspire me.

CREDITS | PERMISSIONS

The Mapping of Love and Death, cover by Andrew Davidson

Maisie Dobbs from the original *Maisie Dobbs* book cover:
Cover of *Maisie Dobbs* courtesy of Soho Press, New York, NY

Covent Garden: Licensed courtesy of the Museum of London,
photographic collection

Lambeth children playing: Licensed courtesy of the Museum of London,
photographic collection

Fitzroy Square: *Robert Adam & His Brothers: Their Lives, Work &
Influence on English Architecture, Decoration and Furniture* (1915),
Wikimedia Commons

MG motor car: Image licensed from Alamy Photographic Agency

Fenwick of Bond Street advertisement: Image licensed from
Alamy Photographic Agency

Elegy for Eddie, cover by Andrew Davidson

Pashley Manor Gardens: Photograph courtesy of Kate Wilson at
Pashley Manor Gardens, Ticehurst, East Sussex

Leaving Everything Most Loved, cover by Andrew Davidson

London tube: Hulton Archive/Archive Photos/Getty Images

An Incomplete Revenge, cover by Andrew Davidson

Messenger of Truth, cover by Andrew Davidson

Pardonable Lies, cover by Andrew Davidson

World War I nurse: From a 1917 painting by Harrington Mann, courtesy
of the Lost Art of Nursing Museum, Cannon Beach, OR